SUE PICKFORD is a British artist of Hong Kong Chinese origin. She specialised in Illustration for her Higher Diploma in Advertising, and worked as an Art Director in the advertising industry for ten years. She is now a creative manager, while also writing and illustrating children's books, and has a second picture book published with Frances Lincoln – *When Angus Met Alvin*. Sue lives with her husband and rescue moggy in Dorset.

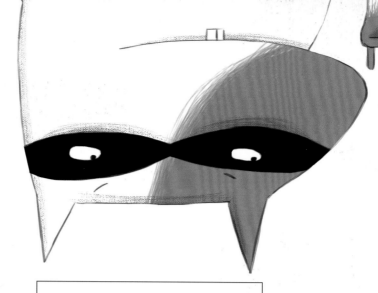

For David, Rhian, Wayne and whoever is about to enjoy this book!

JANETTA OTTER-BARRY BOOKS

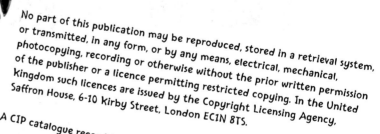

First published in Great Britain in 2013 and in the USA in 2014 by Frances Lincoln Children's Books, 74-77 White Lion Street, London N1 9PF
www.franceslincoln.com

First paperback published in Great Britain in 2014

A CIP catalogue record for this book is available from the British Library.

ISBN 978-1-84780-409-9

Illustrated with pencil, acrylic and digital media

Printed in China

9 8 7 6 5 4 3 2 1

Hur, hur!

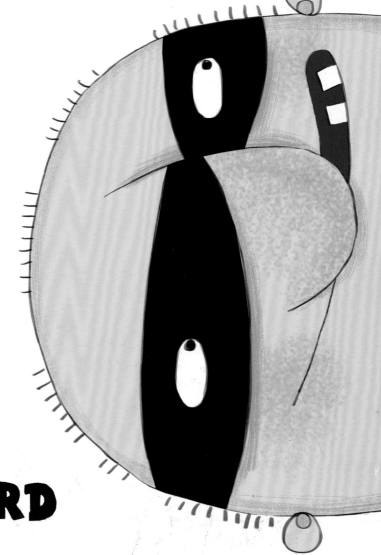

BOB AND ROB

SUE PICKFORD

F
FRANCES LINCOLN
CHILDREN'S BOOKS

Rob loved anything shiny, expensive and preferably stolen. Because he was a burglar and he was bad! Really BAD! He was so bad that he liked to:

leave banana skins on pavements,

"Whoops-a-daisy, how clumsy of ya!"

ring people's doorbells,

and set off fire alarms.

and he baked the most *spectacular* cakes.

And he was taught by his mum always to be faithful to his owner.

Yes, even if he **was** a burglar.

Every evening when the sun went down, Bob and Rob put on their masks and set off to find loot.

But Rob wasn't just bad, he was a bad burglar too.

One day, at a burglar's dog convention, Bob told everybody what he thought.

"Honestly, Rob is going to get us caught one day. A dog's place should be in front of a nice log fire, not in a prison cell!"

Bob was sad, but he decided to forget his dreams of ever becoming a normal dog. After all, he had to remain faithful to his owner, even if he **was** a burglar.

Then one night, while out on the prowl, Bob and Rob spotted a **huge** pile of presents. And what's more, the window was open.

"Hey, talk about easy pickings!" sniggered Rob. "Keep an eye out while I grab this lot."

So while Bob kept guard, Rob stuffed the whole lot into his sack as quickly as he could.

Then they both scurried off into the darkness.

But when they got home,
Rob got a nasty surprise.

"They're all blinkin' toys!

Cheapy, plasticy,

nasty, tacky,

rubbishy, horrid toys.

What a waste of time! Pah!"
He stormed off and went to bed.

"Oh bother," thought Bob. "Some poor children will be crying their eyes out if they don't get these presents tomorrow. I should really take them back."

So he put them all back into the sack, made sure Rob was snoring away nicely and...

heaved them back to where they came from,
huffing and puffing the whole three miles.

HOOT
HOOT
HOOT!

He crept through the window and unloaded all the toys carefully, one by one. But by the time he'd finished, he was so tired that he fell asleep on the spot.

Early next morning he was woken
by a tight **squeeze** round his neck.

Acgghhh...

"Oh no, sorry Rob, please stop!" he choked,
thinking Rob had found him and was trying
to strangle him. "I can explain everything,
honest...acghh!"

Then he saw the faces of three small children.
They were all trying to hug him at once.

"Oh, Mummy, this is the best present ever!"

Can we keep him? PLEASE!"

"Well, if no one comes to claim him, then yes, of course!" **said Mum.**

HOUND FOUND
Very well behaved!
call: 088 088 088

That day posters were stuck on to
every tree in the neighbourhood.

"Hmmm, he sure is the spitting image of Bob
but he can't be, because he looks too GOOD!"
grumbled Rob.

So

no one

came

to

get

him.

Bob was very happy.
He was never bad again.

And neither was Rob.

(Well, not for a while anyway!)

ALSO BY SUE PICKFORD
PUBLISHED BY FRANCES LINCOLN CHILDREN'S BOOKS

WHEN ANGUS MET ALVIN

What would you do if a bossy alien crash-landed his spaceship in your garden
and flattened all the flowers? Show him how to behave, that's what!
A very funny story about friendship and problem-solving.

978-1-84780-304-7

Frances Lincoln titles are available from all good bookshops.
You can also buy books and find out more about your favourite titles,
authors and illustrators on our website: www.franceslincoln.com